kind

imaginative

P9-DHK-595

bitty ☆ baby
makes a
splash

by Kirby Larson
& Sue Cornelison

☆ American Girl®

Special thanks to Dr. Laurie Zelinger, consultant,
child psychologist, and registered play therapist.
Dr. Zelinger reviewed and helped shape the "For Parents"
section, which was written by editorial staff.

Published by American Girl Publishing
Copyright © 2014 American Girl

Questions or comments? Call 1-800-845-0005,
visit **americangirl.com,** or write to Customer Service,
American Girl, 8400 Fairway Place, Middleton, WI 53562-0497.

Printed in China
14 15 16 17 18 19 20 21 LEO 10 9 8 7 6 5 4 3 2 1

Series Editorial Development: Jennifer Hirsch & Elizabeth Ansfield
Art Direction and Design: Gretchen Becker
Production: Jeannette Bailey, Judith Lary, Paula Moon, Kristi Tabrizi

For Jennifer and Holli,
and "the buddies"—
Brynn, Kelsey, and Clair

K.L.

For all his patience, kindness, love,
and support, I dedicate this book to
my husband, Ross.

S.C.

"Let's try on our new swimsuits!" I said. I put on mine and helped Bitty Baby into hers.

"I'm ready for guppy lessons," I told Mommy.

"You don't have to wait too much longer," said Mommy. "They start tomorrow night."

I swam around the kitchen. "I'm a mermaid!"

"What beautiful mermaid arms," said Mommy.

"And you're going to have mermaid hair, too," my brother said, "because you have to put your face in the water."

"In guppy class?" I asked.

"All the way in." My brother pretended to jump into a pool. "Glub, glub," he said.

I went back to my bedroom and took off my swimsuit. Bitty Baby wanted hers off, too.

"I don't think I can put my face in water," I said. "What if it gets in my eyes?"

"Or up your nose?" asked Bitty Baby.

I ran to find Mommy. "Do I have to put my face in the water in guppy class?" I asked.

"Yes," said Mommy. "But the teacher will be right there, helping you."

I curled up on the window seat and hugged Bitty Baby close. "I don't want to go to guppy class."

"But what about the water park this summer?" asked Bitty Baby. "You can't go if you can't swim."

"I don't care," I said. "I'm going to tell a story instead."

"Will there be swimming in it?" asked Bitty Baby.

"There might be," I said.

One day, Bitty Baby packed her treasure bag and set off for the pond. She hadn't gone very far when she met six little ducklings. They were all quacking so loudly that she had to cover her ears.

"What's going on here?" she shouted.

Mr. Duck waddled over. "I'm trying to teach my ducklings how to swim, but they're afraid to follow me into the pond."

"No swimming, no swimming!" cried the ducklings.

"Ducks are supposed to swim," Bitty Baby told them. "That's why you have webbed feet."

"But we don't want to put our heads in," they quacked. "We might get water up our bills!"

Bitty Baby looked at the ducklings. "Do you like treasure hunts?" she asked, pulling a jewel out of her bag.

"We love treasure hunts," quacked the ducklings.

Bitty Baby tossed the
jewel into the water.
"Who's going to hunt
for this treasure?"
she asked.

"Not me!" cried five little ducklings.

"Me, me!" quacked one little duckling. He jumped into the pond and began to paddle.

"Right web, left web. Right. Left," coached Mr. Duck, swimming close behind the little duckling.

"Ready for the treasure hunt?" asked Bitty Baby.

The little duckling wiggled from bill to tail. "Ready."

Mr. Duck counted. "One, two, quack!"

The little duckling dived down. He got the jewel and popped back up. "I did it!"

"Doesn't that look like fun?"
Bitty Baby asked the other ducklings.
"We're scared! We're scared!" they quacked.

"We'll be right here to
help you." Bitty Baby
held up the jewel.
"Who's next?"

One by one, the other
ducklings waddled into
the pond, until finally
even the last duckling
was swimming.

Mr. Duck flapped his wings. "Great job, ducklings," he said. "Let's try diving together. Ready? One, two, quack—everybody under!"

All afternoon, Bitty Baby played with the ducklings. They gathered snails and mudbugs. She gathered jewels for her treasure bag.

"It's time for me to go," she said. "But I'll come back soon!"

And she packed up her treasure bag and went home. The end.

"I like that story," said Bitty Baby. "The baby ducks practiced until they could swim like Mr. Duck."

I thought about how much fun I could have at the water park. "I'm going to practice, too."

I told Mommy my idea and put on my swimsuit. Mommy ran a big bath. I climbed into the tub.

First, I leaned over and blew bubbles. No water got in my eyes. Or up my nose. I leaned back and tried paddling, like the ducklings.

"Right web, left web,"
said Bitty Baby.
"Good job!"

"Thanks." I practiced
my mermaid arms.
"Now I'm ready.
Count to three."

Bitty Baby counted:
"One, two—"

"Quack!" I said.

And under I went.

For Parents

Bath Time!

Most kids love being in water, and baths are no exception. In fact, a bath can be a great way to cheer up a cranky or tired child. But sometimes bath time poses unexpected challenges. Maybe at her last bath the water disappeared down the drain with a gurgly noise, and now your daughter imagines there's a monster in the drain—or that she might go down the drain, too! Or maybe she just doesn't want to stop playing. Here are some ways to keep bath time happy and safe.

Anticipate

As bath time approaches, build some excitement. Say, "Soon it will be time to play in the bath.

Do you think you'll be a dolphin, a mermaid, or a sea turtle today?" If she expresses reluctance, try to get to the root of the problem. Ask her why she doesn't want to take a bath, and show respect for her feelings by taking her answers seriously. If she's afraid of the drain, try using a simple rubber drain cover, and remind her that you'll be there, too. Does she worry about getting soap in her eyes? Bring her some goggles or a plastic visor, and help her create a silly, foamy hairstyle using mousse or shampoo, to go with her headgear.

Focus on Fun

Bath time is playtime with water toys and games. Show her how to make beards or hats out of bubble-bath foam. If she doesn't like having her

hair washed, try working up a good lather using tear-free baby shampoo and then sculpting her hair into animal features: a rooster comb, horse ears and forelock, a lion mane, droopy puppy ears, and so on. She'll be having too much fun to notice that she's getting her hair washed at the same time!

Safety Tips

* Before she gets in, check the temperature of the water with your wrist. It should be warm but not hot. As bath time progresses, test the temperature of the water, running warm water as needed to make sure she doesn't get chilled.
* Place a nonslip mat or decals at the bottom of the tub, and discourage your little one from standing up during bath-time play. Install a rubber faucet cover over your bathtub tap, too.
* Last but not least, **never leave a child unsupervised in the bath,** even if she is playing in just an inch of water. If you need to leave the room, say to answer the phone or doorbell, wrap her in a towel and bring her with you. You can always return to bath time later.

For more parent tips, visit
**americangirl.com/
BittyParents**